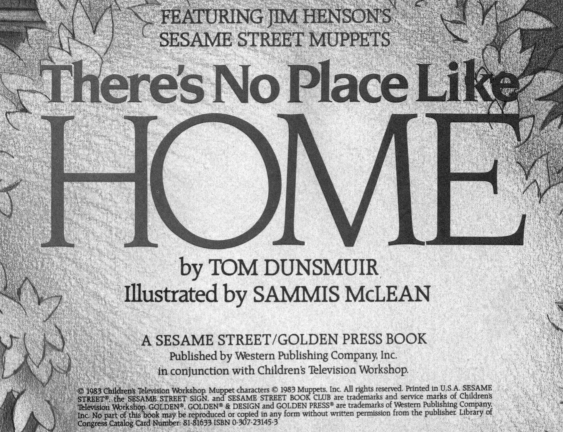

FEATURING JIM HENSON'S
SESAME STREET MUPPETS

There's No Place Like
HOME

by TOM DUNSMUIR
Illustrated by SAMMIS McLEAN

A SESAME STREET/GOLDEN PRESS BOOK
Published by Western Publishing Company, Inc.
in conjunction with Children's Television Workshop.

Everybody lives somewhere.

Some people live in apartment houses in the city. Many families live in the same building.

Some people live in
farmhouses in the country.
Their neighbors live
far away.

I live in a lighthouse on a rocky
island in the middle of the water.

I live on a houseboat. I can catch
my dinner from the window. At night
the waves rock me to sleep.
There's no place like home.

Some people can take their homes
with them wherever they go.

Big deal! I can take my house
with me wherever I go, too.
And I don't have to pay for gas!

I live in an old house with many rooms
and secret places where I can play hide-and-seek.

I live in a brand-new house. There aren't many places to hide, but there's lots of room to paint a big painting.

I built my own log cabin. I did it with my own two hands.

We built our own treehouse.
We did it with our own four hands.

My home has a pointy roof.

My home has a flat roof.

My home doesn't have any roof at all, but I don't care. There's no place like home.

Some houses
are made of wood.

Some houses
are made of brick.

Some are
made of stone.

Others are
made of glass.

And some are made of a kind
of clay called adobe.

I live in a castle with two thousand and twelve bats!

I live in a cottage with my eight curious cats.

I live in a house that is underground
and is heated by the sun.

I live in a cave underground with no heat.
But I have my shaggy coat to keep me warm.

There's a special house where forest
rangers sometimes live. It's called
a lookout station.

There's a special house where the President lives. It's called The White House.

Wherever you live,
there's no place like home.

ABCDEFGHIJKL